# Jamie Lee Curtis's
# Books
## to
# Grow By
## Treasury

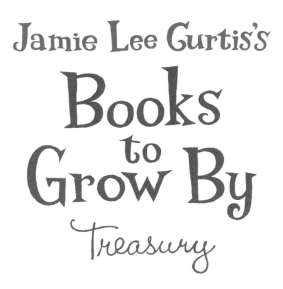

# Jamie Lee Curtis's

# Books to Grow By

## Treasury

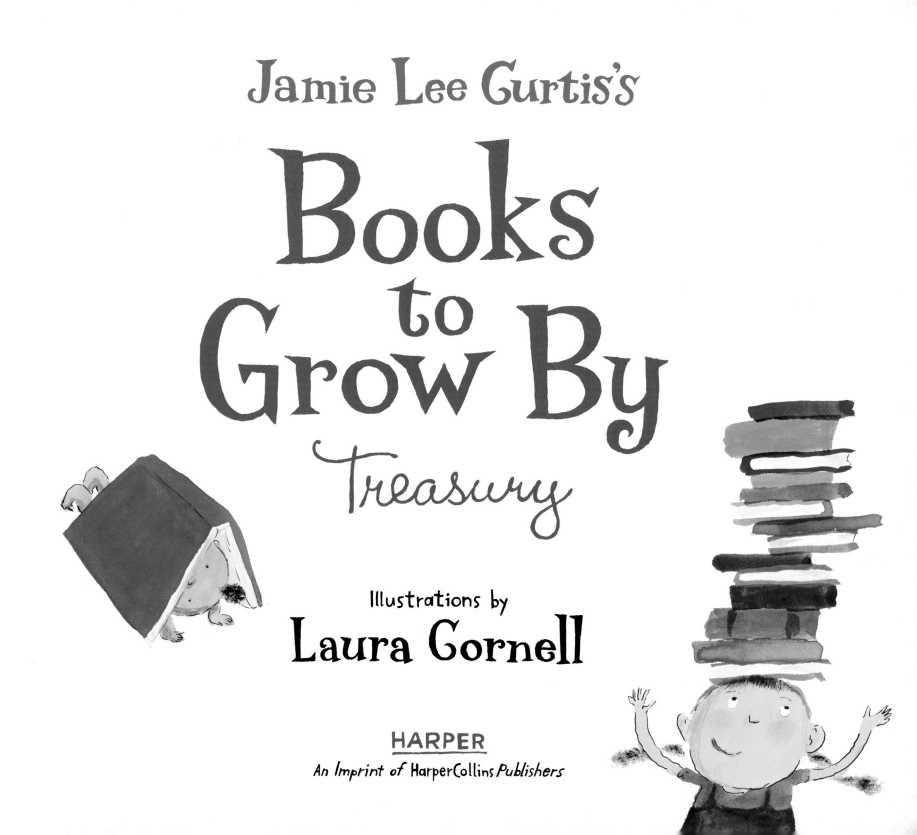

Illustrations by

# Laura Cornell

HARPER

*An Imprint of HarperCollins Publishers*

When cooking or making crafts, it is important to keep safety in mind. Children should always ask permission from an adult before cooking or using scissors and should be supervised by an adult in the kitchen at all times. The publisher and author disclaim any liability from any injury that may result from the use, proper or improper, of the recipe and activities contained in this book.

Jamie Lee Curtis's Books to Grow By Treasury

Text copyright © 1993, 2000, 2002, 2006, 2009 by Jamie Lee Curtis  Illustrations copyright © 1993, 2000, 2002, 2006, 2009 by Laura Cornell

Library of Congress Catalog Card Number: 2008944197  ISBN 978-0-06-180364-2

Typography by Carla Weise 09  10  11  12  13  SCP  10  9  8  7  6  5  4  3  2  1  ❖  First Edition

For Leah Komaiko—our muse, our
hero—for bringing us together

# What's Inside?

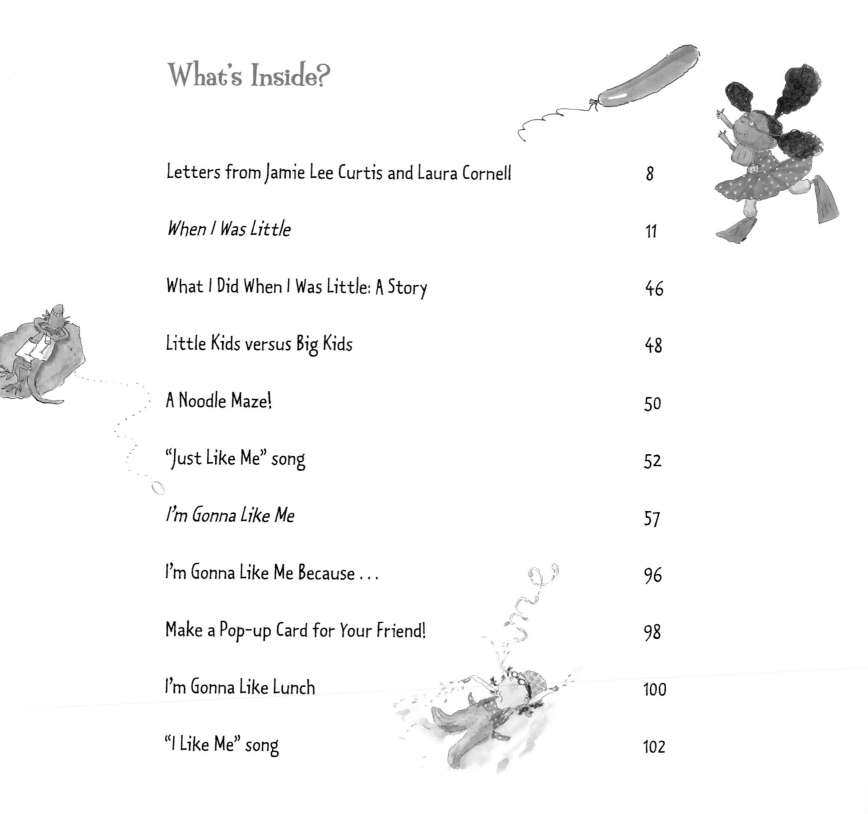

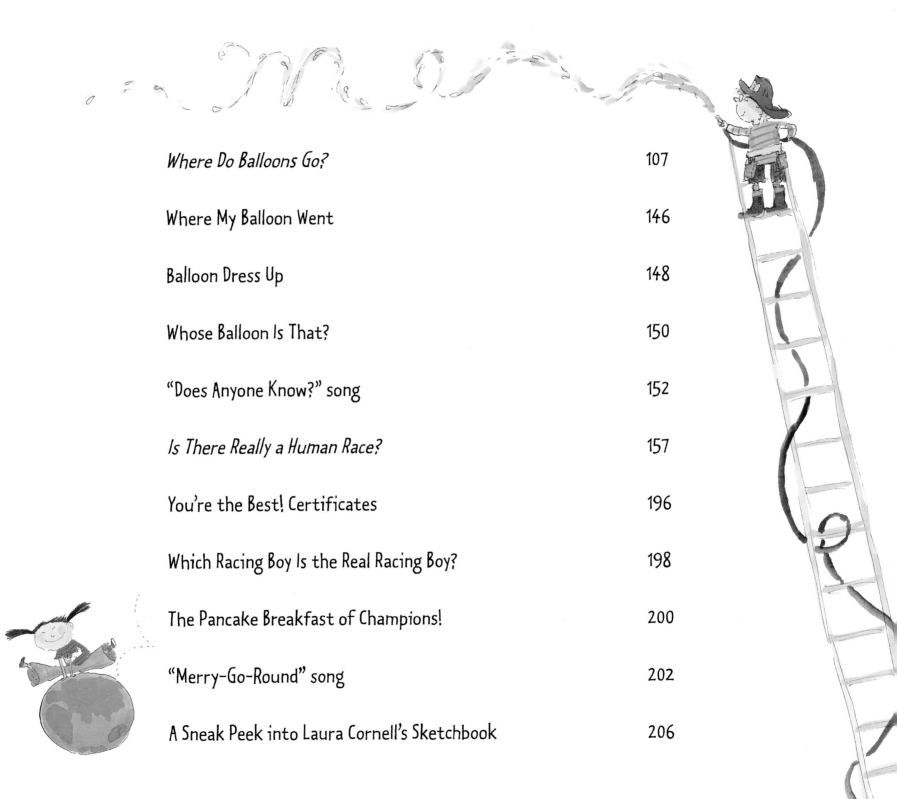

Many years ago my beautiful, cherubic four-year-old daughter, Annie, stomped into my office and proudly declared, "When I was little, I wore diapers and now I use a big girl potty." After she left and I stopped laughing, I casually wrote down on a pad *When I Was Little: A Four-Year-Old's Memoir of Her Youth.* That too made me laugh, thinking that a four-year-old had a past, the good old days. I then started listing accomplishments, and the list ended with three statements that brought tears to my eyes. I realized it was a book for children. The ensuing years have brought me immeasurable joy, great personal satisfaction, and the creation—with the invaluable work of my partner, Laura Cornell—of eight books to grow by for children and their families.

I never intended to become a writer, let alone to write "self-help books for kids." In my writing I really just try to relate to and rejoice in the myriad experiences of a young life and a young mind.

The hope was always that they might be bound in a collection, a portable toolbox, for families to enjoy together. I am thrilled that we are producing this volume and hope that it is merely the first of many.

There is nothing quite like connecting to children from their point of view. If they feel seen and heard by me, and they know that I understand the glorious, harrowing, confusing, and exhilarating life of a child, then I have done my job well.

I hope you enjoy these books together.

As an illustrator, I feel incredibly lucky to have been given the gift of Jamie's wonderful texts.

Jamie's books are thoughtful and funny, full of big ideas and words of compassion and wisdom. With each text comes the opportunity to create a story in pictures. Who are the characters, what do they look like, how do they dress, what are their interests? What do I surround them with that makes them unique? I am inspired by the best of childhoods that my parents gave me, as well as the antics of my daughter, Lilly. Although my California neighborhood and my daughter's Central Park playground are a generation and miles apart, they share the hilarity and endless creativity of kids left to devise their own entertainment.

Thrown into the mix are humorous observations of the characters in my daily life and a loving yet decidedly unsentimental view of it all. Jamie embraces this, even when the pictures seem to run counter to the heart and tenderness of her words. The words and illustrations are, in a way, the perfect partnership of opposites, created by two adults who remember oh so well what it was like to be a kid.

It's wonderful to see four of our books together in a collection with songs, activities, and games. This is exactly the kind of book I would have loved as a kid. I hope you do, too!

*Laura Cornell*

# When I Was Little

## A Four-Year-Old's Memoir of Her Youth

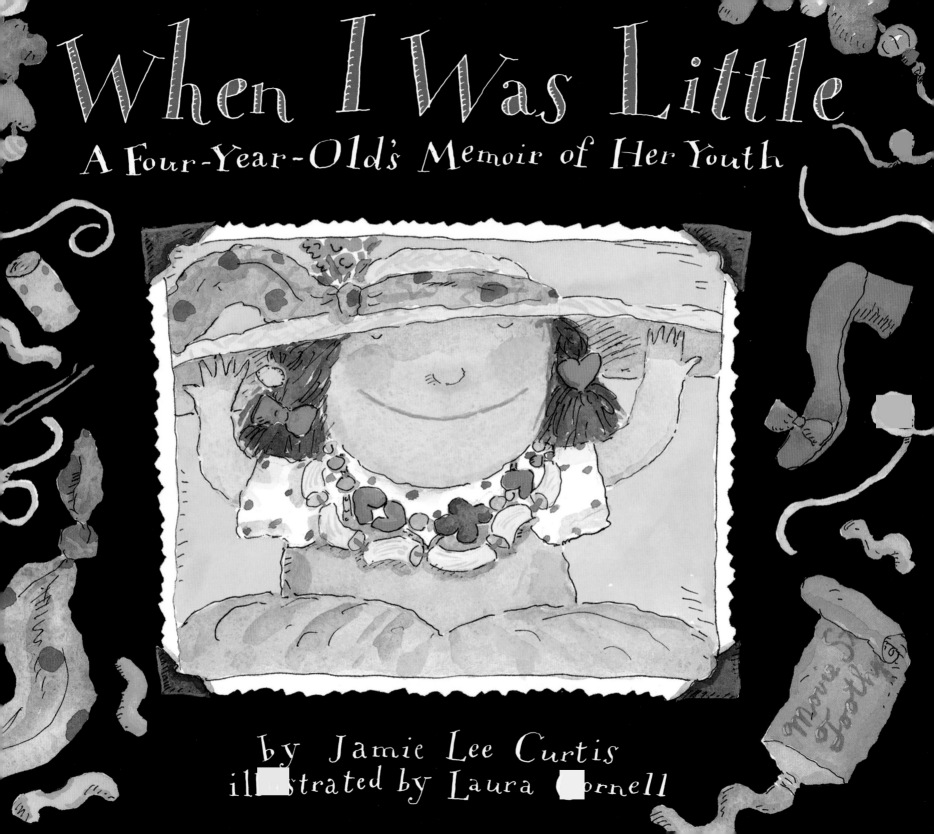

by Jamie Lee Curtis

illustrated by Laura Cornell

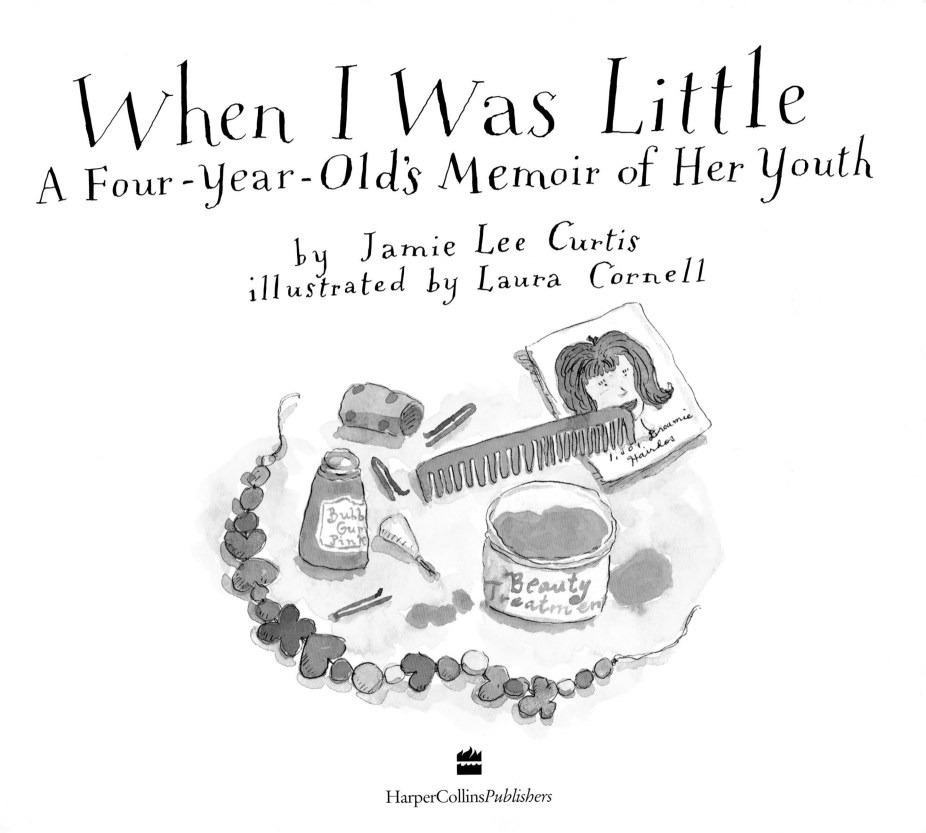

# When I Was Little
## A Four-Year-Old's Memoir of Her Youth

by Jamie Lee Curtis
illustrated by Laura Cornell

HarperCollins*Publishers*

The author wishes to thank Phyllis, Joanna, Marilyn, Laura,
her family, and always, Chris

When I Was Little
A Four-Year-Old's Memoir of Her Youth
Text copyright © 1993 by Jamie Lee Curtis
Illustrations copyright © 1993 by Laura Cornell www.harpercollinschildrens.com

Library of Congress Cataloging-in Publication Data
Curtis, Jamie Lee, date
    When I was little; a four-year-old's memior of her youth / by Jamie Lee Curtis; illustratd by
Laura Cornell.
    p.  com.
    Summary: A four-year-old describes how she has changed since she was a baby.
    ISBN 978-0-06-021078-6 (trade bdg.) — ISBN 978-0-06-021079-3 (lib. bdg.)
    ISBN 978-0-06-443423-2 (pbk.)
    [ 1. Babies—Fiction.   2. Growth—Fiction. ]  I. Cornell, Laura, Ill.   II. Title.
PZ7. C948Wh   1993                                                                91-46188
[E]—dc20                                                                                CIP
                                                                                        AC

For Annie
~J.L.C.

For Lilly
~L.C.

When I was little, I was a baby.

17

When I was little, I cried a lot.
Now I use words.

18

No

When I was little, I didn't know I was a girl.
My mom told me.

When I was little, I had silly hair. Now I can wear it in a ponytail or braids or pigtails or a pom-pom.

When I was little, I didn't get to eat Captain Crunch or paint my toenails bubble-gum pink.

CAP'N CRUNCH

Bubble-G Pink

the Big News

When I was little, I spilled a lot.
My mom said I was a handful.
Now I'm helpful.

When I was little, I rode in a baby car seat.
Now I ride like a grown-up and wave at
policemen.

HAVE YOU SEEN OUR PRECIOUS FI-FI?

REWARD

When I was little, I went to Mommy and Me.

Now I go to nursery school and I have teachers and cubbies and naptime and secrets.

When I was little, I didn't understand time-outs.
Now I do, but I don't like them.

29

*scoopeeloo*

When I was little, I made up words like "scoopeeloo."
Now I make up songs.

When I was little, I swam in the pool with boys. I still do, but now we wear bathing suits but we don't wear floaties.

When I was little, the slide at the park was so big.

Now it's smaller, but I still like my granny to wait at the bottom for me.

35

When I was little, I ate goo and yucky stuff.

Now I eat pizza and noodles and fruit and Chee-tos.

When I was little, I had two teeth.
Now I have lots, and I know how to brush
them.

When I was little, I slept in a zoo. Now I sleep in a big bed and get to play monkey.

When I was little, I kissed my mom and dad good night every night.
I still do, but only after they each read me a book and we play tickle torture.

When I was little, I didn't know what a family was.

When I was little, I didn't know what dreams were.

When I was little, I didn't know who I was.

43

Now I do!

# What I Did When I Was Little: A Story

In *When I Was Little*, a four-year-old tells us all about what she was like as a baby. You can write your own story about what you were like as a baby, too, and how things are different now that you're big. All you have to do is get some paper and crayons (or pencils or markers) and follow the fill-in-the-blanks story written here. A grown-up can help you write it out. Don't forget to draw pictures, too.

Page 1: When I was little, I was a baby. I said _____ all the time. Now I say _____ instead.

Page 2: When I was little, I ate _____ for breakfast. Now I like to eat _____.

Page 3: When I was little, I _____ all day. Now I _____.

Page 4: When I was little, I wore _____.

Now my favorite outfit is _____.

Page 5: When I was little, I didn't know _____.

Now I know _____.

Page 6: When I was little, my bed looked like a

_____.

Now it looks like _____.

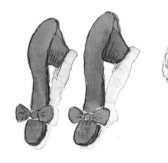

Page 7: When I was little, I went to sleep at _____.

Now my bedtime is _____.

Page 8: When I was little, I couldn't go to sleep unless _____.

Now I _____ before bedtime.

Page 9: When I was little, I dreamed about _____.

Now sometimes I dream about _____.

Page 10: I liked being little because _____.

But the best thing about being big is _____.

# Little Kids versus Big Kids

Little kids and big kids get to do different things, play with different toys, eat different food, and wear different clothes. Can you tell which of these pictures are for big kids and which are for little kids?

Big Kids: bike, shoes, slide, pizza; little Kids: swing, stroller, baby food, booties

# A Noodle Maze!

Oh, no! The little girl from *When I Was Little* can't find her baby brother.
Can you help her get through the maze of noodles so she can take him
home with her?

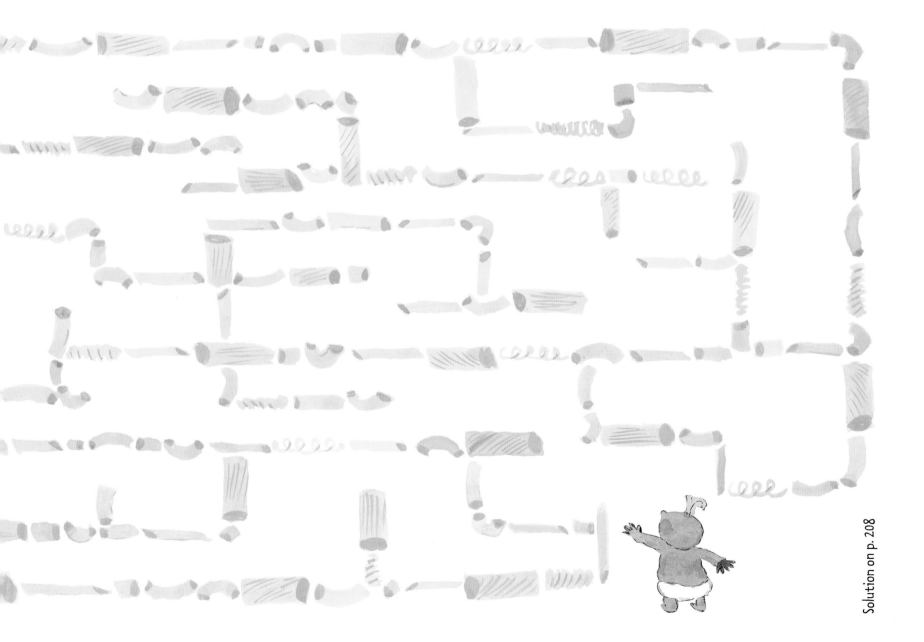

Solution on p. 208

# Just Like Me

Music by Tom Porter
Lyrics by Tom Porter and Daniel Sheerin

Hey lit - tle bro - ther, lit - tle sis - ter, how you've just be - gun.

I re-mem-ber a time just like you, I was turn-ing one. I could-n't talk, could bare-ly walk,

Mom and Dad did ev'-ry -thing. But now I'm al-most four, I can sing and dance a-round in rings; see.

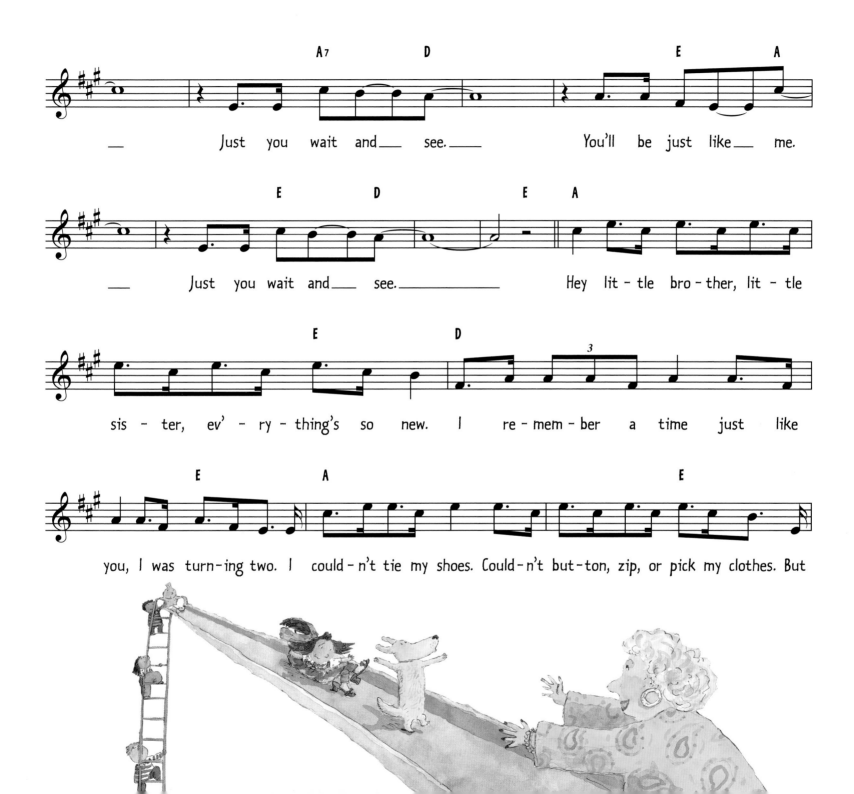

_ Just you wait and_ see._ You'll be just like_ me.

_ Just you wait and_ see._ Hey lit - tle bro - ther, lit - tle

sis - ter, ev' - ry - thing's so new. I re - mem - ber a time just like

you, I was turn - ing two. I could - n't tie my shoes. Could - n't but - ton, zip, or pick my clothes. But

now I'm al - most six, I wan - na let you know that you be - long; see.___

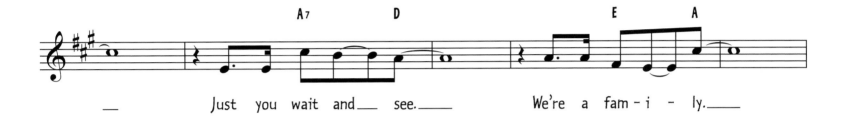

___ Just you wait and___ see.___ We're a fam - i - ly.___

Just you wait and___ see.___ We're a fam - i - ly.___

Just you wait and___ see.___ We're a fam i - ly.___

# Jamie Lee Curtis & Laura Cornell

# I'm Gonna Like Me

## Letting Off a Little Self-Esteem

# I'm Gonna Like Me

## Letting Off a Little Self-Esteem

### by Jamie Lee Curtis

### illustrated by Laura Cornell

Joanna Cotler Books
*An Imprint of HarperCollinsPublishers*

I really like Laura, Joanna, Phyllis and Heidi
(and their many helpers). –J.L.C.

Thank you, every time, Jamie, Joanna, Justin, Jessica,
Alicia, Lucille and Peter.
–L.C.

I'm Gonna Like Me: Letting Off a Little Self-Esteem

Text copyright © 2002 by Jamie Lee Curtis  Illustrations copyright © 2002 by Laura Cornell

For information address HarperCollins Children's Books, a division of HarperCollins Publishers,
10 East 53rd Street, New York, NY 10022. www.harpercollinschildrens.com
Library of Congress Cataloging-in-Publication Data  Curtis, Jamie Lee, date.
I'm gonna like me: letting off a little self-esteem ; by Jamie Lee Curtis ; illustrated by Laura Cornell.—first ed.
p.    cm.  Summary: A young girl learns to like herself every single day, no matter what.
ISBN 978-0-06-028761-0 (trade bdg.) – ISBN 978-0-06-028762-7 (lib. bdg.)
[1. Self-esteem—Fiction.  2. Conduct of life—Fiction.]  I. Cornell, Laura, ill.  II. Title.
PZ8.3.C9344  Im  2002  [Fic]—dc21  2002001300
Designed by Alicia Mikles ❖

For Boco —J. L. C.

For Dennis, Gregory, Martin, Michael, the three Thomases,
Vincent, Walter and Fred —L.C.

I'm gonna like me
when I jump out of bed,
from my giant big toe

to the braids on my head.

I'm gonna like me

when I grin and I see

Sympathy

MODERNE

First Plane RIDE

The Art of Flower Arranging

The Art of Shell Flowers

FROM THIS TO THIS

EXERCISING Your ILLEGAL Turtle

TURTLE MUSIC PELLETS

MEET THE AUTHOR

TRUCKER gods HEART of AMERICA Inspirational Stories for Young Women

Esther Williams actress—water Sprite Inspirational Stories for Young Women

CLARA BARTON BUSY NURSE Inspirational Stories for Young Women

BATHING CAPS through the Ages

Nurse Shoes through the Ages 1950's

A Collection of Fins Wearable METICULOUS DETAIL INCLUDES DORSAL PECTORAL VENTRAL TAIL TUNA GUPPY PIRANHA ANGEL SHARK TROUT

EASY VELCRO COMFORTABLE FOR LONG-WEARING GILLS BONUS: Attachable

65

the space in my mouth
where two teeth used to be.

SP♦T
REMOVER

67

I'm gonna like me
wearing flowers and plaid.
I have my own style.
I don't follow some fad.

as the bus pulls away and I'm feeling so brave.

I'm gonna like me
when I'm called on to stand.
I know all my letters
like the back of my hand.

I'm gonna like me
when my answer is wrong,
like thinking my ruler
was ten inches long.

I'm gonna like me when I'm sharing my lunch

76

I'll twist and I'll stretch

straight up to the sky.

I'm gonna like me
when I fall and get hurt
and mess up my elbows
in pebbles and dirt.

Then they pick teams and I'm chosen last.

I'm gonna like me
when I do the right thing
and return what I found
even when it's a...
RING.

MEDAL OF Bravery

MEDAL OF Intelligence

MEDAL OF Adult Cute

MEDAL OF Suave

I'm gonna like me when I'm feeling strong. I'll walk with a smile, arms swinging, legs long.

1. Catch 150 to 200 lb. octopus.

I'm gonna like me

when I eat something new

2. Clean well.

3. Cook in large pot on stove top.
Season well.
Stir now and then.

4. Serve with rooster foot salad and snail bread.

even if Grandma makes

octopus stew.

I'm gonna like me when I make a mistake and put out the candles on Dad's birthday cake.

I'm gonna like me
when I open the box
and smile and say "Thanks"
even though I got socks.

I'm gonna like me when I try a new task.

I bring in a plate before I am asked.

I'm gonna like me

when I clean in a flash

and play with my brother

and take out the trash.

I'm gonna like me
when I cuddle up tight
and know as I'm sleeping
I'm safe and all right.

I'm gonna like me
'cause I'm loved and I know it,
and liking myself
is the best way to show it.

I'm gonna like me.
I already do!
But enough about me—
How about

# I'm Gonna Like Me Because . . .

There's something special about everyone. In fact, there's usually more than one special thing.

Can you name ten things that you like about yourself and make you feel special?

Here's a start:

I'm gonna like me because . . .

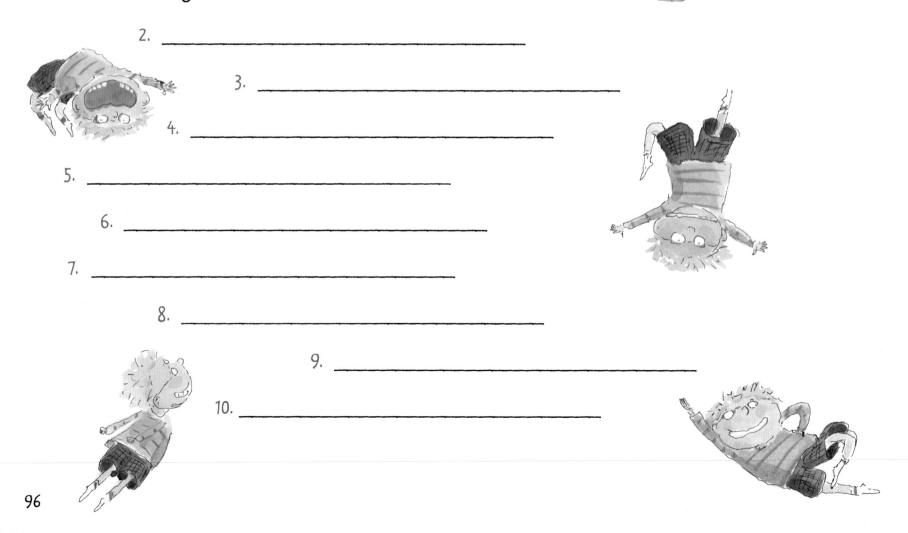

1.  I like listening to stories.

2.  _____

3.  _____

4.  _____

5.  _____

6.  _____

7.  _____

8.  _____

9.  _____

10.  _____

Can you come up with special reasons why you like different members of your family, too?

1. _____

2. _____

3. _____

4. _____

5. _____

6. _____

7. _____

8. _____

9. _____

10. _____

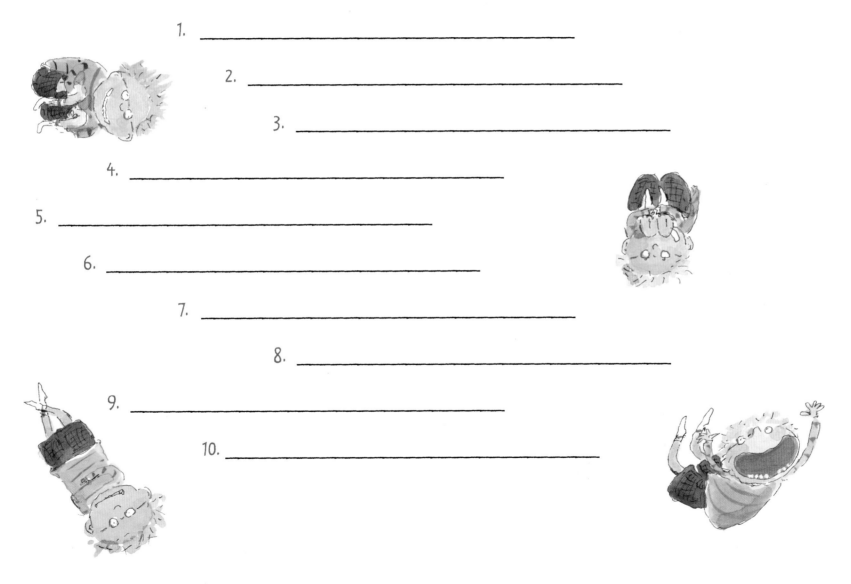

# Make a Pop-up Card for Your Friend!

In *I'm Gonna Like Me*, one of the characters makes a get-well card for her sick friend, Tom. You can make a card just like hers for your friend, too, either for a special occasion, or just to say how much you like being friends.

What you need:

2 pieces of paper (contrasting colors are nice)

Crayons or markers

Scissors (make sure a grown-up helps you with these)

Glue

- One cookie (half-eaten)
- Three cupcakes (two with frosting, one without)
- One fireman (you can't eat him!)
- Three sandwiches
- One juice box (with milk inside)
- One thermos (shaped like a fire hydrant)
- Two pairs of glasses (you can't eat these either!)
- One pair of chopsticks

Solution on p. 208

# I'm Gonna Like Lunch

In *I'm Gonna Like Me*, the characters share their lunches with one another. There are tons of things in their lunch boxes! Can you find all these things in the picture below?

# What to do:

1. Fold a piece of paper in half.
   This is going to be the base of your card.

2. Fold a second piece of paper in half.
   This is going to be your pop-up heart.

3. Draw half of a heart on the edge of the second piece of paper, where it's folded together (see the image on the right). The half heart should be no wider than half the width of the folded paper.

4. With your scissors, cut the heart from the bottom about halfway up. Then use your scissors to cut the curve from the top—but leave half an inch of space between your two cuts so that your heart can pop out.

5. Open the paper up and pop the heart out from the fold.

6. Use the glue to stick your pop-up heart paper onto the inside of your base card, lining up the center folds. Glue down everything but your heart!

7. Decorate the card with markers or crayons, making sure to write your message inside.

8. Now your card is all ready to give to your friend.

_ I rec - om - mend you try, too._____ When I mess up my math

_ in ___ class ___ I laugh, I like me.____ I ___ like ___ me. _____

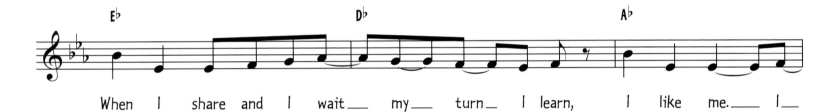

When I share and I wait ___ my ___ turn ___ I learn, I like me.____ I___

_ like ___ me. ____ I'm real - ly hap - py I do. _____

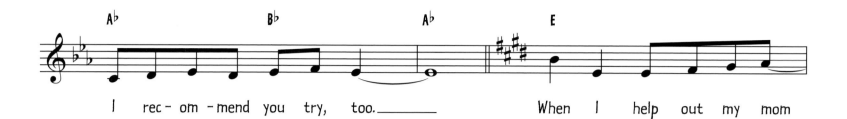

I rec – om – mend you try, too._____ When I help out my mom

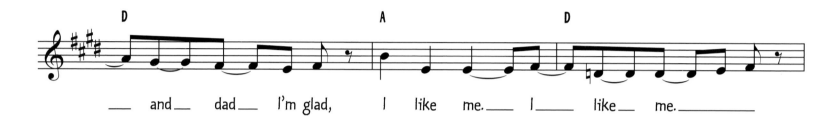

___ and___ dad___ I'm glad, I like me.____ I____ like___ me._____

When I know that I'm all_____ I_____ need___ to be,

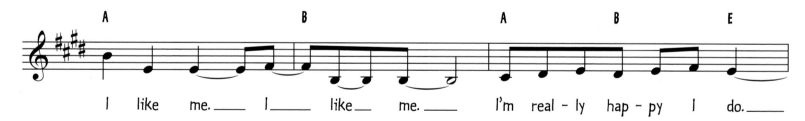

I like me.____ I____ like___ me.____ I'm real – ly hap – py I do.____

I rec - om - mend you try, too._____

*instrumental bridge*

I like me. I_____ like_____ me._____ I like me. I_____

_____ like_____ me._____ I like me. I_____ like_____ me._____

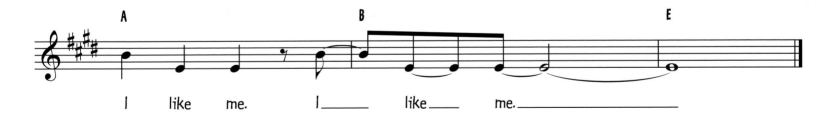

I like me. I_____ like_____ me._____

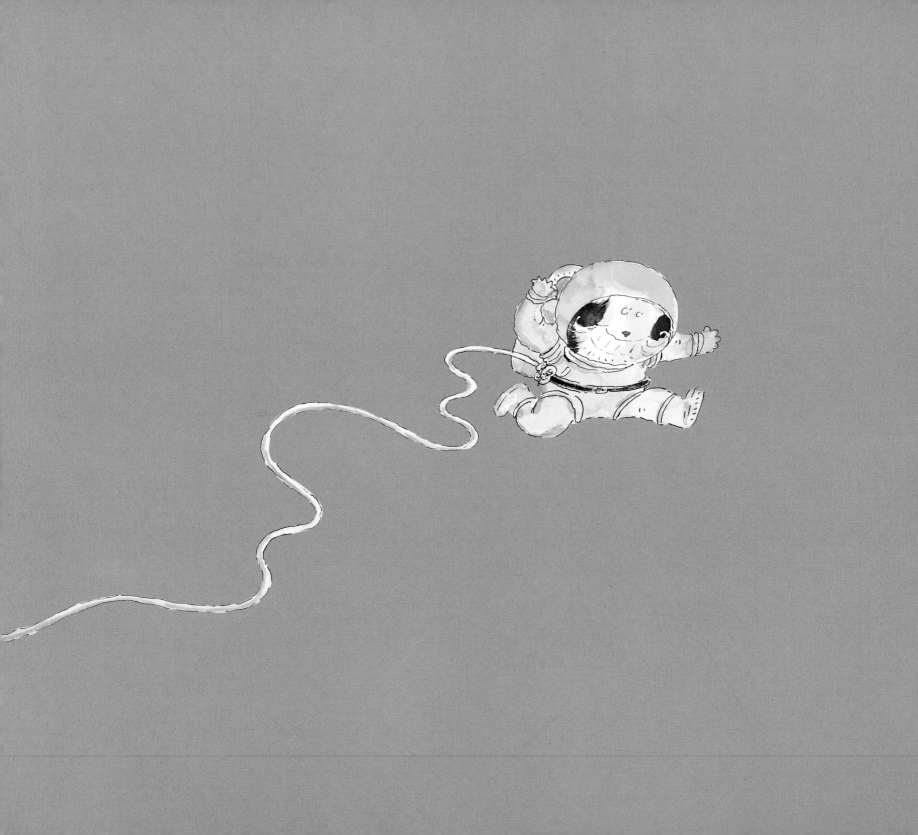

For Tom.
And Rick, in absentia.
~ J.L.C.

For Peter, who leaves me
alone but is always there.
~ L.C.

Where do balloons go
when you let them go free?
It can happen by accident.

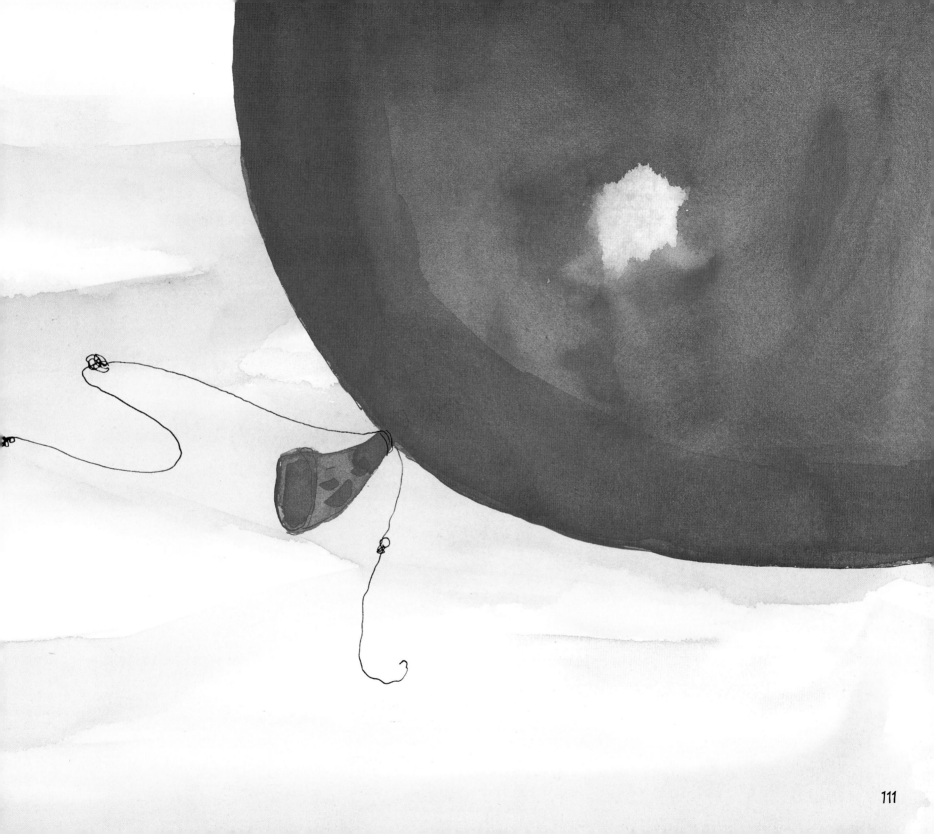

Where do they go
when they float far away?

Do they ever catch cold
and need somewhere to stay?

Do they keep going up?
Can they ever just stop?
I'm sure that they're always
concerned that they'll POP–
        maybe caught up in wires
            pushed by the breeze
                poked by tall buildings
                    or tangled in trees?

Are they always alone?
Do they meet up in pairs?

Do they ever get married
and make balloon heirs?

119

# Do they ever write postcards, e-mail or fax?

Forty-fifth Annual Rubber Convention, Airville, home of famous Hot Air Springs and the wading pool.

Dear Zu Zu,

Enjoying the rubber samples and hot air treatments. Keeping full and shiny.

Wish you were here. See you soon on Main Street.

AIR MAIL
(ha!)

Miss ZuZu Zapateria
1200 Main Street

USA

20¢ USA

Do they ever just let down their strings and relax?

Maybe they're better away from the smog

being twisted by clowns

or chased by my dog.

But floating so high
without worries or cares
don't they miss birthdays,
parties and fairs?

Where do balloons go?
What's really up there?
As far as I see,
it's just sky and air.

125

Do they tango with airplanes?

Or cha-cha with birds?

Care to dance?

Can plain balloons read
balloons printed with words?

If one's loose in Norway
and one in Tibet
and one in Alaska
and Mass-a-chu-SETTS

and one in Bolivia,
England and France

do they all meet up high

MONA'S
MONSTER
SHOP

Dr. Chas
COLLAGEN
1(800) LIPS

BALLOON

Do some go so far
that they end up in space?
Do they challenge the rockets
to float them a race?

OTTO'S AUTO PARTS

Sparky SPACE CRAFTS

OFFICIAL
SATURN ON LEFT
EARTH ON RIGHT
SHOOTING STARS
INTERMITTENT
QU
ACTI

SPACE GUIDE
BIG DIPPER STRAIGHT
AHEAD
METEORS NOW AND THEN
BLACK HOLES HARDLY EVER
WATCH OUT FOR BALLOONS

Fine dining
at
SPACE LOUNGE
air conditio
for your
com fr

STOP GO

DOW

BEYOND OZONE
1 BILLION + SPF

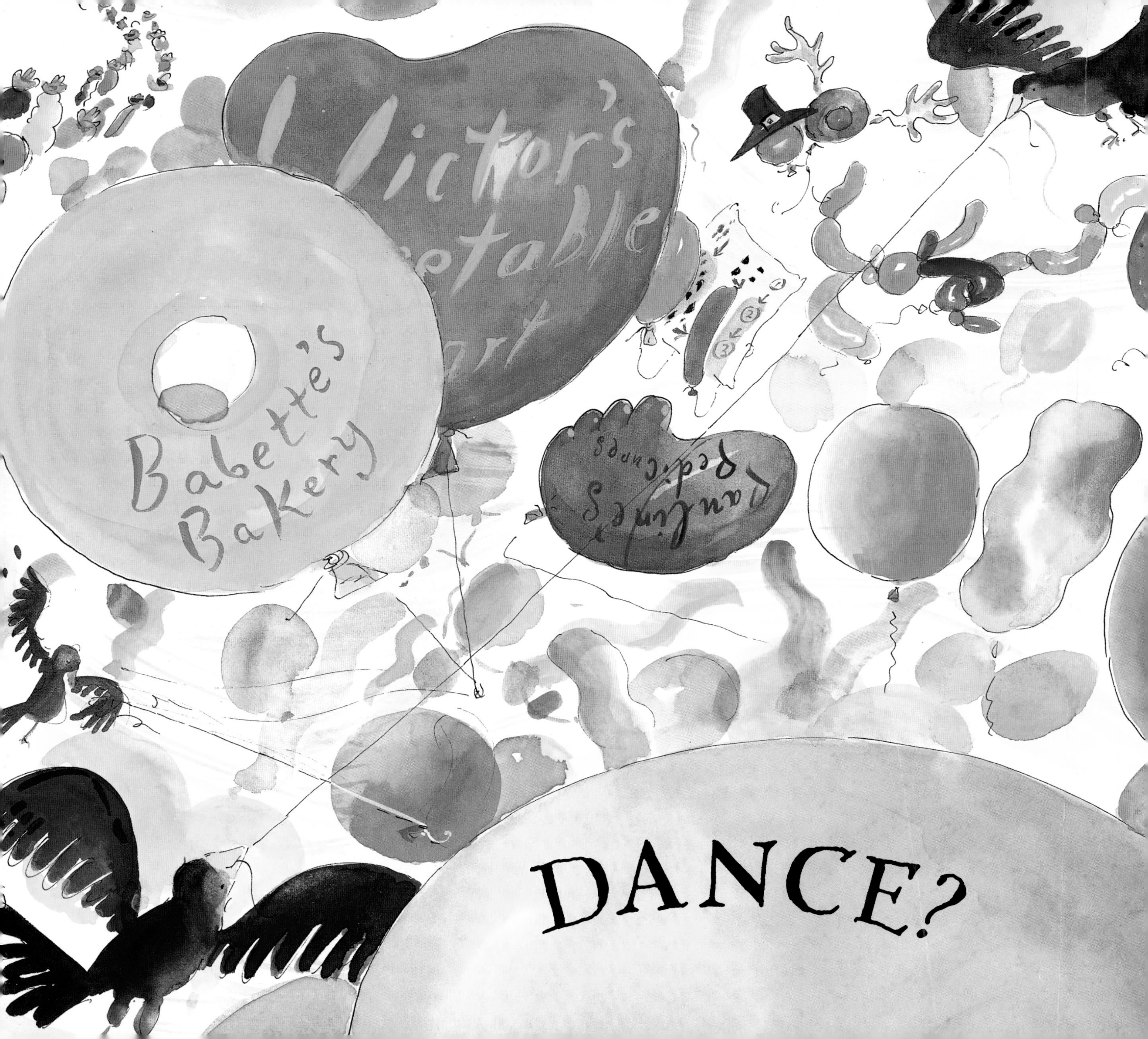


DANCE?

Then does it get quiet?
Do the stars give a shove?
And send it on high
to that place up above?

And what if the leader
gets close to the sun?
We know rubber melts.
That wouldn't be fun.

Does it float there forever
remembering me?
And know that I'm happy
that it's floating free?

SCAR KIT

REAL LOOKING
MONSTER SCARS

5 VARIETIES

SCRUFFY DOG

Where _do_ balloons go?
It's a mystery, I know.
So just hold on tight
till you have to

let go.

143